Please Say PLEASE!

KYLE T. WEBSTER

Scholastic Press • New York

LIBRARY OF CONGRESS CATALOGING-IN-PUBLICATION DATA
Webster, Kyle T., author.
Please say please! / Kyle T. Webster. — First edition.   pages cm
Summary: In rhyming text, a little girl learns the importance of saying please when she asks
for anything. ISBN 978-0-545-84485-7 (hardcover : alk. paper) 1. Courtesy — Juvenile
fiction. 2. Stories in rhyme. [1. Stories in rhyme. 2. Etiquette—Fiction.] I. Title.
PZ8.3.W394Pl 2016   [E] — dc23   2015024362

10 9 8 7 6 5 4 3 2 1   16 17 18 19 20
Printed in Malaysia 108   First edition, August 2016
The type was set in Century Schoolbook, Twentieth Century, and Behemoth Serif Condensed.
Book design by Kyle T. Webster, Charles Kreloff, and David Saylor

WISHES GRANTED TO THOSE WHO SAY PLEASE!

For Hermione & Wolfie

Please say
"PLEASE,"
and you'll
brighten
my day.

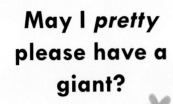